STONE ARCH BOOKS
a capstone imprint

STONE ARCH BOOKS™

Published in 2015 by Stone Arch Books
A Capstone Imprint
1710 Roe Crest Drive
North Mankato, MN 56003
www.capstonepub.com

Originally published by DC Comics in the U.S. in single magazine form as The All-New Batman: The Brave and the Bold #3
Original U.S. Editor: Scott Peterson

DC Comics
1700 Broadway, New York, NY 10019
A Warner Bros. Entertainment Company

Library of Congress Cataloging-in-Publication Data

Fisch, Sholly, author.
Through the looking glass! / Sholly Fisch, writer ; Rick Burchett, penciler ; Dan Davis, inker ; Heroic Age, colorist.
pages cm. -- (The all-new Batman: the brave and the bold ; 3)
"Originally published by DC Comics in the U.S. in single magazine form as The All-New Batman: The Brave and the Bold #3."
"Batman created by Bob Kane."

Summary: Trapped in a wacky Wonderland filled with white rabbits and Cheshire cats, Batman and The Flash have to battle a pair of villains to find their way back to the real world.
ISBN 978-1-4342-9660-3 (library binding)
1. Batman (Fictitious character)--Comic books, strips, etc. 2. Batman (Fictitious character)--Juvenile fiction. 3. Flash (Fictitious character)--Comic books, strips, etc. 4. Flash (Fictitious character)--Juvenile fiction. 5. Superheroes--Comic books, strips, etc. 6. Superheroes--Juvenile fiction. 7. Good and evil--Comic books, strips, etc. 8. Good and evil--Juvenile fiction. 9. Graphic novels. [1. Graphic novels. 2. Superheroes--Fiction. 3. Characters in literature--Fiction. 4. Fantasy.] I. Burchett, Rick, illustrator. II. Kane, Bob, creator. III. Title.

PZ7.7.F57Tj 2015
741.5'973--dc23

2014028252

STONE ARCH BOOKS
Ashley C. Andersen Zantop Publisher
Michael Dahl Editorial Director
Eliza Leahy Editor
Heather Kindseth Creative Director
Bob Lentz Art Director
Peggie Carley Designer
Katy LaVigne Production Specialist

Printed in China by Nordica.
0914/CA21401510
092014 008470NORDS15

THE ALL NEW!
BATMAN
THE BRAVE AND THE BOLD
THROUGH THE LOOKING GLASS
SHOLLY FISCH ....WRITER
RICK BURCHETT...............................PENCILLER
DAN DAVIS..INKER
HEROIC AGE....................................... COLORIST
BATMAN created by
Bob Kane

A TEAM-UP BETWEEN THE MIRROR MASTER AND THE MAD HATTER IS BIZARRE ENOUGH--
--BUT MIRROR MASTER, MAD HATTER, AND THE ORIGINAL FLASH?!
WHY NOT? HE IS ONE OF THE FEW HEROES WITH THE GOOD TASTE TO WEAR A HAT!
THE HATTER MUST BE CONTROLLING THE FLASH'S MIND! WE HAVE TO FREE HIM--QUICKLY!

SURE--
--BUT WHICH ONE DO WE FREE?

JAY GARRICK WAS THE FLASH BEFORE MY PARTNER TOOK OVER THE ROLE.
USUALLY, THERE'S ONLY ONE OF HIM.
MIRROR, MIRROR...
SHOLLY FISCH • WRITER RICK BURCHETT • PENCILLER DAN DAVIS • INKER
HEROIC AGE • COLORISTS TRAVIS LANHAM • LETTERER CHYNNA CLUGSTON FLORES • ASST. EDITOR
SCOTT PETERSON • EDITOR BATMAN CREATED BY BOB KANE

THAT ONE! KEEP HIM BUSY--
--AND KEEP HIM IN ONE PLACE!
WHY THAT ONE?
THE LIGHTNING BOLTS ON THE OTHERS' CHESTS ARE BACKWARD. THEY'RE MIRROR IMAGES.
THIS FLASH IS THE REAL ONE.

THERE. WITHOUT THE MAD HATTER'S MIND-CONTROL CIRCUITRY, HE SHOULD BE BACK TO NORMAL IN NO TIME.
ARE YOU OKAY?
...B-BATMAN...? FLASH...? W-WHAT...?
DEAR ME! I IMAGINE WE SHAN'T ENJOY THIS NEXT BIT AT ALL.
STICK TO THE PLAN, YE RAVIN' LOONY! JUMP INTO MY MIRROR!
COME ON! BEFORE THEY GET AWAY!
WAIT! WE DON'T KNOW WHAT'S WAITING ON THE OTHER...
...SIDE.
SO MUCH FOR PLANNING...

WHOA! LOOKS LIKE WE'RE NOT IN KANSAS ANYMORE!
WRONG BOOK.
WE'RE NOT IN OZ.
BREAD AND BUTTER!
I SAID "HALT!" NOT "TRIP ALL OVER EACH OTHER!" "HALT!"
WE'VE GONE THROUGH THE LOOKING GLASS.

WE FASHIONED THIS ENTIRE LOOKING GLASS WORLD OUT OF THE MIRROR MASTER'S SOLID LIGHT--AND MY GENIUS! ISN'T IT SIMPLY FRABJOUS?
THIS HAS TO BE A DREAM...
AH, BUT WHOSE DREAM? IF YOU WAKE THE WRONG PERSON, YOU MIGHT DISAPPEAR!
AW, THAT'S IMPOSSIBLE.
PERSONALLY, I ALWAYS TRY TO BELIEVE SIX IMPOSSIBLE THINGS BEFORE BREAKFAST.
ZZZZZZZZ
THAT'S ENOUGH, HATTER! GET US OUT OF HERE!
"OUT?" WHY WOULD ANYONE EVER WANT TO GET OUT OF HERE?
SORRY, BATMAN.
HE HASN'T THE SLIGHTEST IDEA HOW TO ESCAPE.
THIS PLACE WAS HIS IDEA, BUT MY WEE MIRROR HERE IS THE ONLY EXIT--
--SO I'LL JUST TAKE IT WITH ME!
WITH YE HEROES STRANDED HERE WITH MY "PARTNER"--
--THERE'S NO ONE T'STOP ME FROM ROBBING CENTRAL CITY BLIND!

MIRROR MASTER'S GONE--VANISHED LIKE A CHESHIRE CAT!
"CHESHIRE CAT?" STUFF AND NONSENSE!
THOSE FILTHY FELINES BELONG DOWN A RABBIT HOLE, NOT THROUGH A LOOKING GLASS!
MMM... YOU TWO HAVE THE LOOK OF KNIGHTS. A RED KNIGHT AND A...DARK KNIGHT?
HMPF! NOT A PROPER KNIGHT AT ALL! PROPER KNIGHTS ARE RED OR WHITE, NOT DARK!
UM, EXCUSE ME, BUT HOW DO WE GET OUT OF HERE?
SILENCE! YOU ARE IN THE PRESENCE OF THE RED QUEEN!
A KNIGHT MAY NOT INTERRUPT A QUEEN!
DON'T MIND HER MAJESTY. WE'LL TALK TO YOU.
PERHAPS YOU'D CARE TO DISCUSS SHOES AND SHIPS AND SEALING WAX?
NO, I--
OR CABBAGES AND KINGS?
AGGGHHH! NEVER MIND, I'LL FIND A WAY OUT MYSELF!

YEESH! THIS PLACE MIGHT ALMOST BE FUN, IF WE WEREN'T TRAPPED HERE.
BUT AT THIS SPEED, I SHOULD FIND US AN EXIT IN NO--
--TIME...?
HOW DARE YOU?
KNIGHTS MUST MOVE IN AN L SHAPE! ONLY QUEENS MAY TRAVEL AS FAR AS THEY WANT, AS QUICKLY AS THEY WANT!
YOU MEAN...LIKE IN CHESS?
A KNIGHT MAY NOT MOVE LIKE A QUEEN!
OFF WITH HIS HEAD!
WHHOOOOOA!
"OFF WITH HIS HEAD" IS A QUOTE FROM ALICE IN WONDERLAND, NOT THROUGH THE LOOKING GLASS.
NOT QUITE ACCURATE, I KNOW. BUT IT'S SUCH A LOVELY SENTIMENT, I COULDN'T RESIST.

I HATE TO DISAPPOINT YOU, GUYS, BUT I'M KIND OF *ATTACHED* TO MY HEAD RIGHT NOW.

GET MOVING! *YOU'RE* GOING TO HELP ME *SAVE* THE FLASH!
PERHAPS--
--OR YOU COULD TRY TO SAVE AN *INNOCENT* INSTEAD!

WHOA!
NO!

HUMPTY DUMPTY!
SOUND THE ALARM!

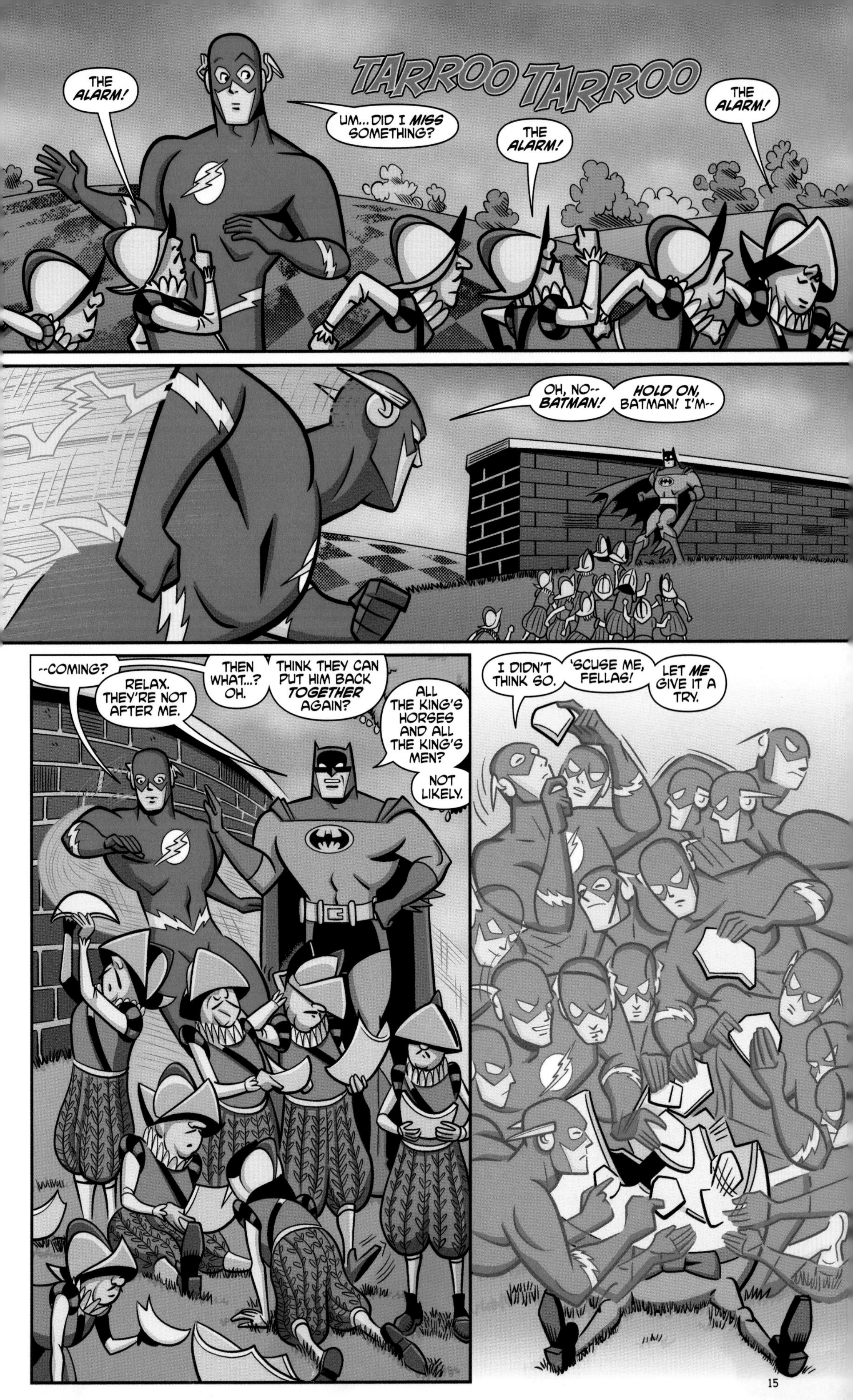

THE *ALARM!*
UM... DID I *MISS* SOMETHING?
TARROO TARROO
THE *ALARM!*
THE *ALARM!*

OH, NO-- *BATMAN!*
HOLD ON, BATMAN! I'M--

--COMING?
RELAX. THEY'RE NOT AFTER ME.
THEN WHAT...? OH.
THINK THEY CAN PUT HIM BACK *TOGETHER* AGAIN?
ALL THE KING'S HORSES AND ALL THE KING'S MEN?
NOT LIKELY.

I DIDN'T THINK SO.
'SCUSE ME, FELLAS!
LET *ME* GIVE IT A TRY.

CAN YOU *VIBRATE* US HOME ACROSS DIMENSIONS?
NOT WITHOUT KNOWING MORE ABOUT WHERE WE ARE. THERE'S NO TELLING *WHERE* WE'D END UP.
NO SIGN OF ANY *OTHER* WAY OUT, EITHER.
THE WAY OUT? IT'S *THAT* WAY!
NO, *THIS* WAY!
THIS WAY!
THIS WAY!
WE'LL *NEVER* GET OUT OF HERE!
NOW, NOW. A ROUTE IS BOUND TO APPEAR *TOMORROW.*
YOU MEAN WE JUST HAVE TO WAIT *ONE DAY?*
OH, NO, NO. WHEN TOMORROW COMES, IT WON'T BE "TOMORROW" ANYMORE. IT WILL BE *"TODAY."*
THEN, YOU SHALL HAVE TO WAIT *ANOTHER* DAY FOR "TOMORROW."

BUT THAT MEANS WAITING *FOREVER!* THAT'S *CRAZY!*
WE'RE *ALL* A LITTLE MAD HERE.
IT COMES WITH *LIVING BACKWARD* IN A LOOKING-GLASS WORLD.

"LIVING BACKWARD...?"
I'M SO CONFUSED...
GOOD!
BREAD AND BUTTER?

HOW IS THAT "GOOD"?
THIS INSANE WORLD WAS BUILT AS ONE BIG *TRAP* FOR US. OVER THE YEARS, I'VE LEARNED THAT *EVERY* TRAP HOLDS THE KEY TO ITS OWN ESCAPE.
TO FIND IT, YOU JUST HAVE TO THINK LIKE THE PERSON WHO *BUILT* THE TRAP.
AIIIEEEEE!

'T-TWAS *B-BRILLIG*... ALL *M-MIMSY* WERE THE BOROGOVES...
W-WHIFFLING THROUGH THE T-TULGEY WOOD!
EYES OF *F-FLAME!*
YOU MEAN THINK LIKE... *HIM?*
WHAT'S HE *TALKING* ABOUT?

BEWARE THE JABBERWOCK, MY SON!
YOU TWO! KNIGHTS!
TAKE THIS VORPAL SWORD AND DEFEND MY PEOPLE!
WE'LL DEFEND THEM--BUT WE WON'T NEED YOUR SWORD.
ONLY A VORPAL SWORD CAN SLAY THE JABBERWOCK!
WE DON'T KILL.

I HOPE YOU'VE GOT A PLAN!
OF COURSE. PROTECT THE BYSTANDERS. STAY ALIVE LONG ENOUGH TO FIND ITS WEAKNESS.
I KNEW I COULD COUNT ON YOU.
BUT ARE YOU SURE THIS THING HAS A WEAKNESS?
ITS HIDE'S SO TOUGH, IT DOESN'T EVEN NOTICE A COUPLE THOUSAND SUPER-SPEED STOMPS!
EVERYTHING HAS A WEAKNESS.
YOU BETTER BE RIGHT, BECAUSE THIS THING IS COMPLETELY OUT OF--
GRROOOOAARRRR!
--CONTROOOOOLL!
WHUFF!
OUT OF...
...THAT'S IT.

TO DEFEAT THE JABBERWOCK, WE HAVE TO THINK LIKE THE PERSON WHO CREATED IT.
COME HERE, HATTER.
OH, DEAR. PLEASE INFORM HER MAJESTY THAT I SHALL BE LATE FOR TEA.
I SEEM TO BE A TRIFLE TIED UP.
FLASH-- CATCH!
THANKS, BUT IT'S THE OTHER FLASH WHO WEARS A HAT--
--OH! GOTCHA!
HOLD STILL, JUMBO!
I JUST NEED A SECOND TO COMPLETE YOUR ENSEMBLE.

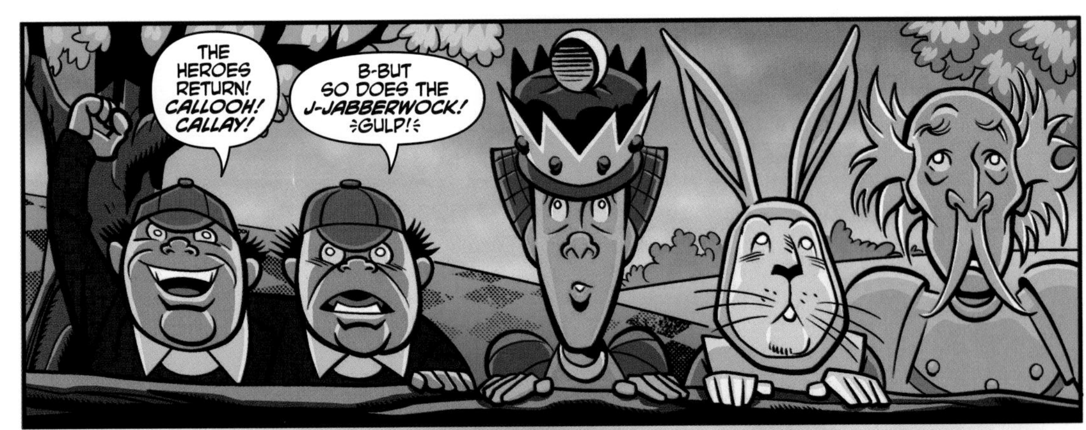

WHAT IS THE MEANING OF THIS? YOU DIDN'T *SLAY* THE JABBERWOCK?

YOU HEARD THE MAN--WE *DON'T* KILL.

THAT IS *MADNESS!*

PROTECTING THE INNOCENT WITHOUT KILLING ISN'T *MADNESS*--IT'S *JUSTICE.*

WITH THE HATTER'S *HAT* AND ONE OF HIS *MIND CONTROL CAPS*--

--I CAN SEND THE JABBERWOCK *FAR, FAR AWAY,* NEVER TO RETURN.

WELL..."NOT KILLING" IS AN *ODD* APPROACH TO JUSTICE. BUT IF IT RIDS US OF THE JABBERWOCK...
OKAY, THAT'S *ONE* PROBLEM DOWN. NOW, IF WE JUST KNEW HOW TO GET *OUT* OF HERE...
OH, I FIGURED *THAT* OUT ALREADY.
ONCE I TRIED THINKING LIKE THE HATTER, THE CLUES WERE *EVERYWHERE.*

WE KEPT MOVING *FORWARD* FROM ONE ENCOUNTER TO THE NEXT. BUT IT'S LIKE THE WHITE KNIGHT SAID--IN A *MIRROR WORLD,* WE NEED TO LIVE *BACKWARD!*
LIVE *BACKWARD?* THAT'S *IMPOSSIBLE!*
"PERSONALLY, I ALWAYS TRY TO BELIEVE *SIX* IMPOSSIBLE THINGS BEFORE BREAKFAST..."

QUITE RIGHT! AS I MENTIONED, A SOLUTION IS BOUND TO APPEAR *TOMORROW.* HOWEVER, IF YOU LIVE BACKWARD, TODAY BECOMES *YESTERDAY,* AND *TOMORROW* BECOMES *TODAY--*
OKAY, OKAY, I'LL TRY *ANYTHING.*
JUST... PLEASE. STOP *EXPLAINING--*IT MAKES MY HEAD HURT.

YEARS AGO, AN OLD YAQUI SHAMAN TAUGHT ME SOME *MEDITATION TECHNIQUES* THAT SHOULD HELP.
JUST DO WHAT I DO.

IN A MIRROR WORLD, TIME NATURALLY FLOWS BACKWARD.
WE'D BEEN MOVING FORWARD OUT OF HABIT.
BUT ONCE WE RELAXED INTO THE NATURAL FLOW OF THIS WORLD...
...WE LIVED BACKWARD THROUGH OUR ENCOUNTERS WITH THE JABBERWOCK, THE RED QUEEN, AND THE OTHERS.
UNTIL...
IT'S WORKING! WE'RE BACK AT THE PORTAL!

AND WE'RE *OUT.*
NOW TO FIND THE *MIRROR MASTER.*
I WOULDN'T WORRY ABOUT IT.

MIRROR MASTER TRAPPED *US* IN THERE--
--BUT HE FORGOT WHO WAS WAITING *OUT HERE!*

OH, THERE YOU ARE.
WHERE HAVE *YOU* FELLOWS BEEN?
YOU'D NEVER BELIEVE IT.
I WOULD.
I ALWAYS TRY TO BELIEVE *SIX* IMPOSSIBLE THINGS BEFORE BREAKFAST...
END

CREATORS

SHOLLY FISCH

WRITER

Bitten by a radioactive typewriter, Sholly Fisch has spent the wee hours writing books, comics, TV scripts, and online material for over 25 years. His comic book credits include more than 200 stories and features about characters such as Batman, Superman, Bugs Bunny, Daffy Duck, Spider-Man, and Ben 10. Currently, he writes stories for Action Comics every month, plus stories for Looney Tunes and Scooby-Doo. By day, Sholly is a mild-mannered developmental psychologist who helps to create educational TV shows, websites, and other media for kids.

RICK BURCHETT

PENCILLER

Rick Burchett has worked as a comics artist for over 25 years. He has received the comics industry's Eisner Award three times, Spain's Haxtur Award, and he has been nominated for England's Eagle Award. Rick lives with his wife and two sons near St. Louis, Missouri.

DAN DAVIS

INKER

Dan Davis has illustrated the Garfield comic series as well as books for Warner Bros. and DC Comics. He has brought a variety of comic book characters to life, including Batman and the rest of the Super Friends! In 2012, Dan was nominated for an Eisner Award for the Batman: The Brave and the Bold series. He currently resides in Gotham City.

GLOSSARY

accurate [AK·yuh·rit]--correct or exact

bizarre [bi·ZAHR]--very strange or odd

bystanders [BYE·stan·durs]--people who are watching an event but not participating

circuitry [SUR·kit·ree]--the plan for or parts of an electric system

ensemble [ahn·SAHM·buhl]--a group of performers

loony [LOO·nee]--crazy or foolish

meditation [med·i·TAY·shuhn]--the act of thinking deeply and quietly

presence [PREZ·uhnss]--being in a place at a certain time

shaman [SHAW·muhn]--a healer who deals with beings in the spirit world

technique [tek·NEEK]--a way of doing something that requires skill

trifle [TRYE·fuhl]--a small amount

weakness [WEEK·nuhss]--something that prevents someone or something from being effective

VISUAL QUESTIONS & PROMPTS

1. Why do you think the artist chose to separate this panel from the rest of the page with a distinct panel border?

2. The sky is different colors throughout the story -- most often a combination of red, pink, orange, and yellow. Why do you think the artist chose to color the sky this way? Would it make a difference if the sky was blue?

3. The Mad Hatter uses a pun -- "tied up" -- when Batman captures him in these panels. How do the text and illustrations work together to make the pun?

4. Batman and The Flash have had enough of Wonderland and are looking for a way out. What is the problem with the White Knight's explanation?

5. Why do you think the Wonderland characters' faces show up in the shards of the mirror in the last panel of the story?

READ THEM ALL!

THE ALL NEW!
BATMAN
THE BRAVE AND THE BOLD

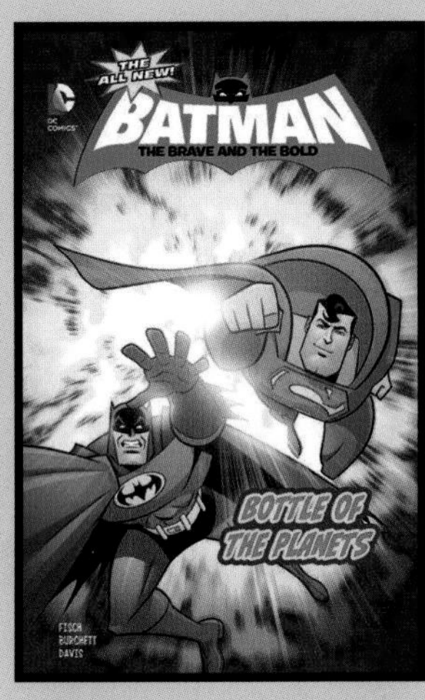
THE ALL NEW!
BATMAN
THE BRAVE AND THE BOLD
BOTTLE OF THE PLANETS
FISCH
BURCHETT
DAVIS

THE ALL NEW!
BATMAN
THE BRAVE AND THE BOLD
THAT HOLIDAY FEELING
FISCH
BURCHETT
DAVIS

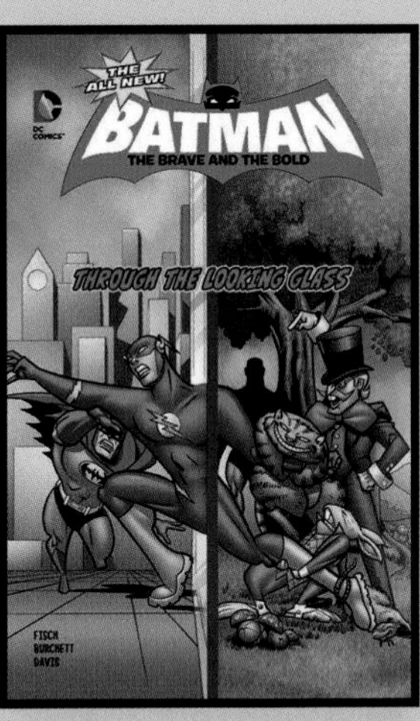
THE ALL NEW!
BATMAN
THE BRAVE AND THE BOLD
THROUGH THE LOOKING GLASS
FISCH
BURCHETT
DAVIS

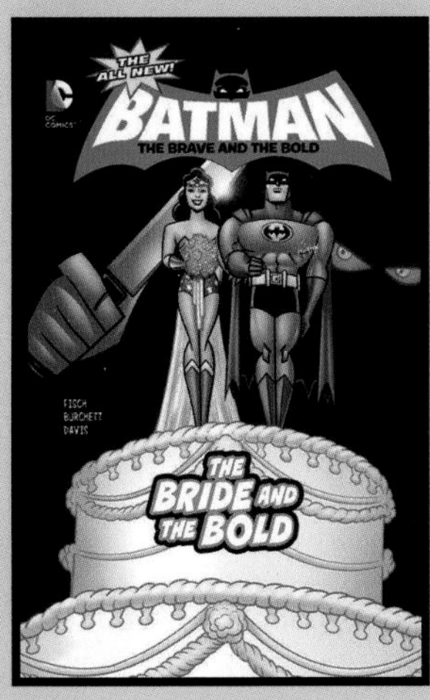
THE ALL NEW!
BATMAN
THE BRAVE AND THE BOLD
FISCH
BURCHETT
DAVIS
THE BRIDE AND THE BOLD

THE ALL NEW!
BATMAN
THE BRAVE AND THE BOLD
FISCH
BURCHETT
DAVIS
MANHANDLED BY MANHUNTERS!

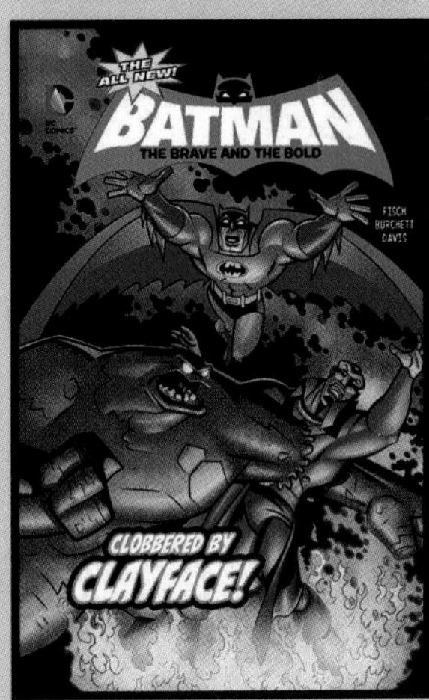
THE ALL NEW!
BATMAN
THE BRAVE AND THE BOLD
FISCH
BURCHETT
DAVIS
CLOBBERED BY CLAYFACE!

THE ALL NEW!
BATMAN
THE BRAVE AND THE BOLD